BAAA

BAAA

David Macaulay

Houghton Mifflin Company Boston 1985

Thanks for various reasons to:
Don Berger
Gerry Craig-Linenberger
Brian Hayden
Walter Lorraine
Ruth Macaulay
David Porter
Chris Van Allsburg
and
Barbara and Marcus Thompson and
all their friends at Seldom Seen Farm.

for
Elizabeth and Charlotte

There is no record of when the last person disappeared. The only person who could have recorded when the last person disappeared was the last person to disappear.

But no matter who left last, the place was deserted.

One day a flock of sheep in a remote pasture ran out
of food. Their search for nourishment took them to an
abandoned town, where they ate the lawns, flower beds,
and potted plants.

Tired of traveling yet still hungry, they wandered
into a house where a refrigerator hummed. Its food was
cold and hard, but the sheep found it quite tasty.

For the next few days, the sheep did nothing but
eat, drink, and sleep. When they ran out of food in one
house, they shuffled into another.

After eating, drinking, and sleeping their way
through seventeen houses, they stumbled into a
supermarket. They couldn't believe their eyes. It was
filled with food.

It was also filled with terrible music, so the sheep
took their favorite items back to the houses.

One day, while gamboling across a family room, a
young lamb accidentally turned on a television. When it
began to glow, everyone stared and stared.

After three days, some of the sheep became bored. They went outside and frolicked in the fresh air. But that became boring too, so they went back inside to watch more glow.

Then, machines were discovered that made
pictures and sounds inside televisions.

By watching movies over and over again, the sheep
learned to speak and eventually to read.

The more they learned about people, the more they
wanted to be like them.

They started wearing clothes and discovered that
many are made of wool (so that's where it went!).

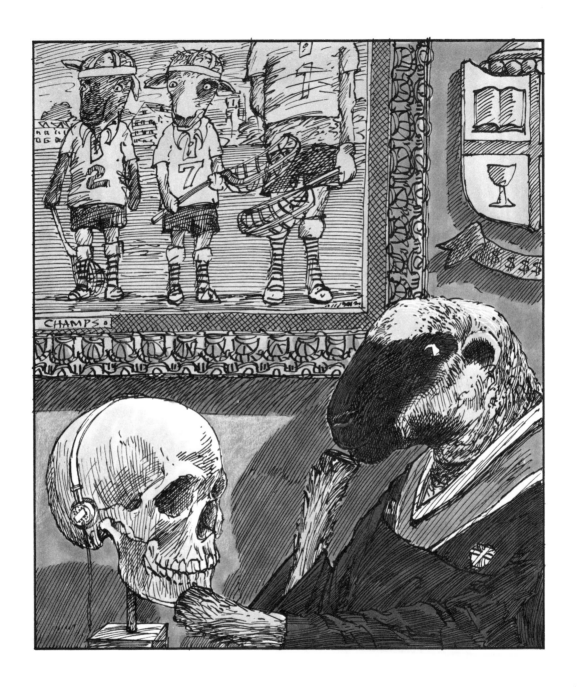

Schools were established. Thoughts were had.

Careers were pursued. Bank accounts opened.

Television stations went back on the air. Some
sheep became quite famous. Even weather sheep.

It was a time of great prosperity. Everything was plentiful. Gas was cheap. The population grew.

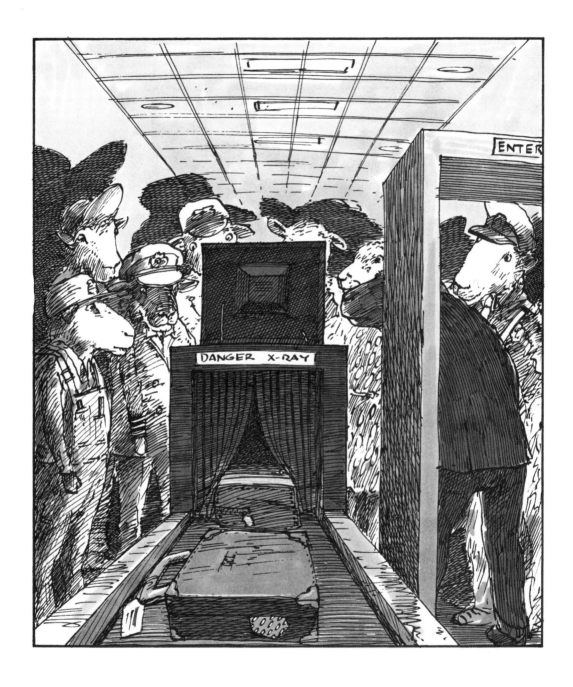

Soon sheep were traveling.

Some went on business trips.

Others sought their roots.

Around this time, leaders arose from the sheep
population. Some had charisma, others connections.

At breakfast time, leaders and other interesting
sheep appeared on television and discussed timely
topics.

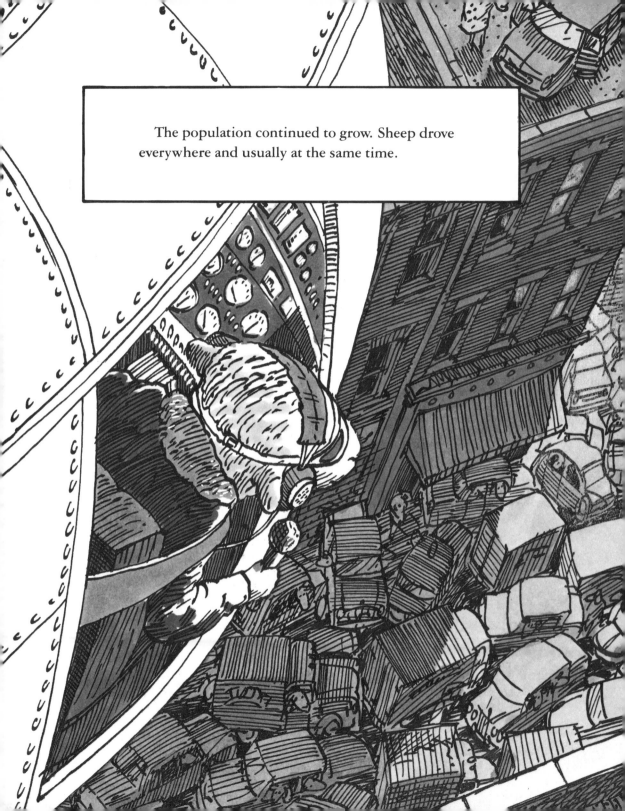

The population continued to grow. Sheep drove everywhere and usually at the same time.

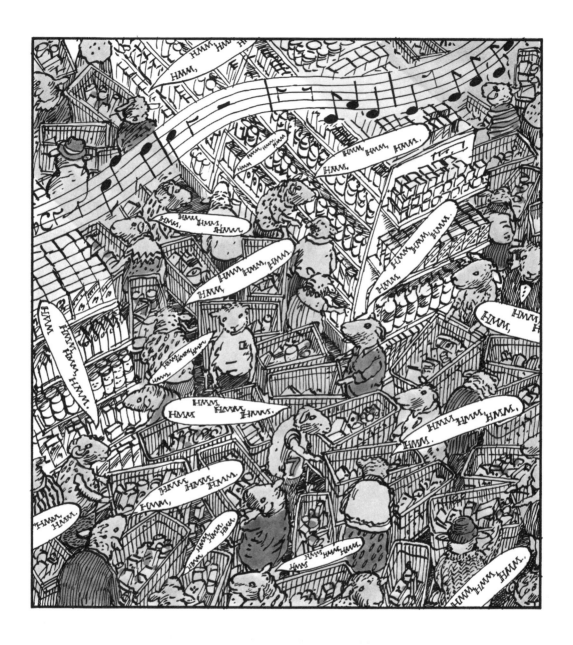

As the good life continued, it naturally became a little more complicated. Lines at markets and gas stations were growing longer and moving more slowly.

Popular items were often gone from the shelves by
ten o'clock in the morning, and for the first time since
they left the pasture, some sheep were going to bed
hungry.

One evening, between commercials, a news sheep
announced that things were being used up too fast.
But nobody paid much attention.

However, when even the leaders couldn't get
everything they wanted, rationing was imposed. After
this, there was almost enough to go around.

Then things got worse, so laws were passed. And
still some neighborhoods always seemed to have more
of everything.

Hungry sheep turned to crime.

As more and more goods went to fewer and fewer
sheep, the number of unhappy sheep grew.

Riots broke out and injuries were sustained. More
comedies were shown on television.

The leaders presented charts and graphs that
proved there was no hunger.

But not everyone heard the good news.

Desperate and angry, a number of sheep marched
into town to see their leaders. Unfortunately, the
leaders were tied up in meetings and could not be
disturbed.

Tempers flared. Terrible words were shouted.
Things were thrown. Troops arrived to keep the peace.

The following day, an end to the food shortage was announced. A new product called *Baaa* had been invented. It would be cheap, plentiful, and nutritious.

Everyone tried it and everyone liked it. Peace
returned. But then everyone liked it too much, and soon
the *Baaa* was all gone. Again, sheep were hungry.
Again, they threw things.

Once more troops restored the peace, and shortly thereafter *Baaa* shops reopened with fresh supplies. For months this process repeated itself.

While the population steadily declined, the demand
for *Baaa* grew.

The trouble persisted and peace had to be restored
a few more times.

By the time the throwing had stopped completely,
Baaa was enormously popular.

Baaa vans were familiar to everyone. They passed
through some neighborhoods several times a day.

Once again, life was comfortable. There wasn't a
single unhappy sheep to be found anywhere.

As the population grew smaller, fewer leaders were
required.

Each evening, more and more houses were
vacant, more televisions cold.

Entire neighborhoods became completely abandoned.

The silence spread. Pools went unfiltered.

With hardly anyone left to lead, the remaining
leaders were unnecessary. They, too, disappeared.

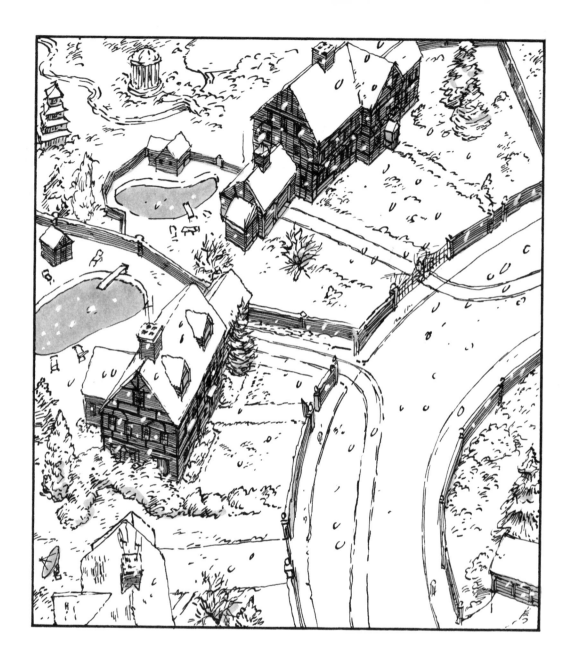

Eventually, there were only two sheep left.

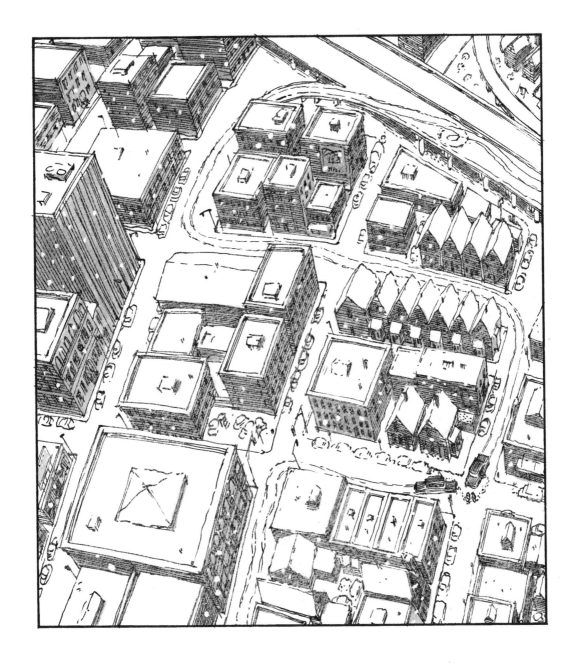

And one day they met for lunch.

There is no record of when the last one disappeared.

Much later, a fish cautiously swam toward the beach. It stared at the land for a long time and then turned and swam in the opposite direction. The next day, it came back and this time swam a little closer to the beach before turning around. It came back several times that week. On the eighth day, it swam almost to the very edge of the water, intending to crawl onto the dry land. But, at the last moment, it turned again and disappeared into the depths of the ocean.

Library of Congress Cataloging in Publication Data

Macaulay, David.
    Baaa.

    Summary: After the last person has gone from
the earth, sheep take over the world, make the same
mistakes as man, and eventually they too disappear.
    [1. Sheep—Fiction. 2. Civilization—Fiction.
3. Allegories] I. Title.
PZ7.M1197Baaa   1985   [Fic]   85-2316
ISBN 0-395-38948-8

Printed in the United States of America

H 10 9 8 7 6 5 4 3 2 1